I Miss You, Stinky Face

Written by:
Lisa McCourt

Illustrated by:
Cyd Moore

Troll
BridgeWater Books

For Tucker...L.M. ⊙ ⊙ ⊙ For Ran and Jay...C.M.

Text copyright © 1999 by Lisa McCourt.
Illustrations copyright © 1999 by Cyd Moore.

Published by BridgeWater Books, an imprint and
registered trademark of Troll Communications L.L.C.

Produced by Boingo Books, Inc.

Printed in the United States of America.

10 9 8 7 6 5 4 3

Library of Congress Cataloging-in-Publication Data

McCourt, Lisa.
        I miss you, Stinky Face / written by Lisa McCourt ; illustrated by Cyd Moore.
                p.   cm.
        Summary: On the telephone to her son, a mother promises the many ways she will come to
rejoin him, traveling by hot-air balloon, camel, cheetah, and shark.
        ISBN 0-8167-5647-3
        [1. Mother and child—Fiction.]   I. Moore, Cyd, ill.   II. Title.
PZ7. M47841445Iah   1999
[E]—dc21   98-31230

"I miss you, my little Stinky Face," said Mama on the phone.
But I had a question.

Mama, do you miss me so much that you're coming right home to me, no matter what?

"I'm coming today," said Mama, "on a big silver airplane."

But, Mama, but, Mama, what if the airplane forgets how to fly?

"If that airplane forgets how to fly, I'll hop in the basket of a hot-air balloon. I'll soar past clouds and stars until I see your window, then I'll float right into your room."

But, Mama, what if the balloon runs out of hot air and you have to land in the middle of the desert?

"If I have to land in the middle of the desert, I'll climb up on a camel and ride him like a racehorse all the way home."

But, Mama, but, Mama, what if the camel gets so tired that he just won't take another step and he leaves you stranded in the jungle?

"Then I'll search that jungle for a cheetah, the fastest animal there is. I'll jump on her back, and she'll race me straight home to you."

But, Mama, what if the cheetah doesn't want to leave the jungle?

"If the cheetah doesn't want to leave the jungle, I'll hunt down some pirates digging for buried treasure and ask them to sail me home to you on their big scary ship."

"Then I'll find the speediest shark in the ocean. I'll grab on to his fin and use it to steer, and we'll skim through the high seas all the way home to you."

"If the shark tries that, I'll leap from his greedy jaws and body surf to shore. I'll call the bravest astronauts and hitch a ride on their supersonic spaceship, and we'll all be home to you faster than the speed of light."

But, Mama, what if their spaceship gets sucked through a black hole and takes you far back in time to a big old castle instead of to our house?

TODAY'S DATE JUNE 20 1262

"If the spaceship lands that far back in time, I'll look around for a magic dragon.

"I'll climb way up on her back and whisper in her ear just how much I miss you. The magic dragon will fly me through time right back to you."

But, Mama, where would such a big magic dragon land?

"I think there's enough room on the driveway if you make
sure your bike's put away."

I'll put it away.... But, Mama, the airplane is
how you'll probably come home, right?

"Probably."

I miss you, Mama.

"And I miss you, my little Stinky Face."